A WRENBOY'

A Wrenboy's Carnival

Gabriel Fitzmaurice

WOLFHOUND PRESS

First published in 2000 by
Wolfhound Press Ltd
68 Mountjoy Square
Dublin 1, Ireland
Tel: (353-1) 874 0354
Fax: (353-1) 872 0207

Available in England, Scotland and Wales
from Peterloo Poets, Cornwall

British Library Cataloguing in Publication Data
A catalogue record for this book is available from the British Library.

ISBN 0-86327-802-7 (paperback)
ISBN 0-86327-845-0 (hardback)

 Wolfhound Press receives financial assistance from
The Arts Council/An Chomhairle Ealaíon, Dublin, Ireland.

10 9 8 7 6 5 4 3 2 1

Cover Illustration: *Wrenboys' Carnival* by Bob Ó Cathail, Baile an
    tSléibhe, Ventry, Co. Kerry, Ireland
Cover Design: Mark O'Neill
Typeset in Classic Garamond by Wolfhound Press
Printed in the Republic of Ireland by ColourBooks, Dublin

In memory of my father and mother,
Jack and Maud Fitzmaurice,
and especially for Brenda, John and Nessa
with love

Other Books by Gabriel Fitzmaurice

Poetry in English
Rainsong (Beaver Row Press)
Road to the Horizon (Beaver Row Press)
Dancing Through (Beaver Row Press)
The Father's Part (Story Line Press)
The Space Between: New and Selected Poems 1984–1992 (Cló Iar-Chonnachta)
The Village Sings (Story Line Press; Cló Iar-Chonnachta; Peterloo Poets)

Poetry in Irish
Nocht (Coiscéim, Dublin)
Ag Síobshiúl Chun an Rince (Coiscéim)
Giolla na nAmhrán (Coiscéim)

Children's Poetry in English
The Moving Stair (The Kerryman)
The Moving Stair (enlarged edition — Poolbeg Press)
But Dad! (Poolbeg Press)
Puppy and the Sausage (Poolbeg Press)

Children's Poetry in Irish
Nach Iontach Mar Atá (Cló Iar-Chonnachta)

Essays
Kerry on my Mind (Salmon Publishing)

Translation
The Purge (A translation of *An Phurgóid* by Mícheál Ó hAirtnéide — Beaver Row Press)
Poems I Wish I'd Written: Translations from the Irish (Cló Iar-Chonnachta)

Editor
The Flowering Tree/An Crann Faoi Bhláth (contemporary poetry in Irish with verse translations) with Declan Kiberd (Wolfhound Press)
Between the Hills and Sea: Songs and Ballads of Kerry (Oidhreacht)
Con Greaney: Traditional Singer (Oidhreacht)
Homecoming/ An Bealach 'na Bhaile (selected poems of Cathal Ó Searcaigh) (Cló Iar-Chonnachta)
Irish Poetry Now: Other Voices (Wolfhound Press)
Kerry Through its Writers (New Island Books)
The Listowel Literary Phenomenon: North Kerry Writers — A Critical Introduction (Cló Iar-Chonnachta)
Rusty Nails and Astronauts: A Wolfhound Poetry Anthology (Wolfhound Press) with Robert Dunbar
'The Boro' and 'The Cross': The Parish of Moyvane-Knockanure (The Moyvane-Knockanure Millennium Book Committee) with Áine Cronin and John Looney

Wrenboy

Wrenboys
(pronounce ran-boys)
— they can be male or female of any age —
celebrate Christmas and Solstice on 26 December
in many villages and parishes in Ireland;
fabulously mortal,
they array themselves in gaily coloured costumes
and go from house to house
singing, dancing, making music, making merry;
nowadays
large groups of 'Wrenboys' form to compete
at various Summer and Harvest Festivals
mainly in the south-west of Ireland.

Acknowledgements

A Wrenboy's Carnival includes poems from the following collections (some poems have been revised since first publication): *Rainsong, Road to the Horizon* and *Dancing Through* published by Beaver Row Press, Dublin; *The Father's Part* published by Story Line Press, Oregon; *But Dad!* and *Puppy and the Sausage* published by Poolbeg Press, Dublin; *The Village Sings* co-published by Story Line Press, Peterloo Poets, Cornwall, and Cló Iar-Chonnachta, Conamara; and *Poems I Wish I'd Written: Translations from the Irish* which was published by Cló Iar-Chonnachta.

'A Parent's Love' and 'In the Woods' first appeared in Irish in *Giolla na nAmhrán* (Coiscéim, Dublin 1998).

A number of these poems were broadcast on RTÉ 1 Television, on Radio Kerry and on RLO (Limerick).

Some of the uncollected poems were published in the following :

An Ríocht, Bricín Poetry Broadsheet, ELF: Eclectic Literary Forum (US), *Fortnight, Markings: The Galway Advertiser, New Series: Departures, Podium, Poetry Ireland Review, Quadrant* (Australia), 'The Boro' and 'The Cross', *The Formalist* (US), *The Kerryman, The Limerick Leader, The Lyric* (US)

My thanks to the editors.

G.F.

Contents

Introduction

The literary career of Gabriel Fitzmaurice is a living illustration of the truth that whenever a country produces a writer of quality, he or she is never quite like the country's official idea of itself. Official Ireland through the 1970s and 1980s devoted itself to rampant Europeanisation. Accession to the European Economic Community in 1973 seemed to demand a determinedly cosmopolitan tone by way of cultural reflex. It became a point of pride for writers to connect with the mind and sensibility of contemporary Europe. Nor was this a singularly Irish obsession. In lands as far apart as Australia and Brazil, artists seemed increasingly indifferent to the pursuit of local or national modes, as they went in search of transnational themes and globalised audiences. By the mid-1980s, the very notion of international solidarity had changed its meaning, having ceased to denote the pooling of national resources and becoming instead an alternative to national culture, an international style. All talk was now of 'world novels' and 'world music' in the new global economy.

It was in the middle of this period of compulsory internationalism that I first came upon the poetry of Gabriel Fitzmaurice. He was reciting it, mostly from memory, in a Listowel pub to an audience composed equally of North Kerry neighbours and visiting Germans. The irony had a sweetness: for here was a poet who had refused to follow the international style actually serving his own community in a time-honoured Irish tradition, but doing so with such integrity that eavesdroppers from a faraway country were held spell-bound. As I listened to the Moyvane man describe in lines of poetry the lore of every local hill and glen, the incidents from history and the meaning of changing placenames, I thought of the old bardic *dinnsheanchas* and of Yeats's prayer that his child be 'rooted in one dear perpetual place'. Fitzmaurice's fidelity to his own village had the sort of magnificent, even reckless, intensity that was deeply moving; and the proof of its enduring value lies in the fact that his own people have always embraced his poetry as warmly as his lines have embraced them.

The next time I heard Fitzmaurice read was almost ten years later, in the attic restaurant of Bewley's Oriental Café in Grafton Street, Dublin. There in the nation's capital his core audience was still his own people, Kerry folk transplanted to the city but still earthed in their own culture; but all around them, like an ineradicable penumbra, once again was to be found a gathering of overseas listeners, not just from continental Europe but from even further afield.

Between those two readings, much had happened in the outside world. The Berlin Wall had come down; the communist tyranny had collapsed; and compulsory internationalism was at an end, while the youth of the world learned once again how to savour indigenous cultures without shame or apology. Now all the talk was no longer of the dirigiste state but of re-vitalising the community: from Tony Blair to Václav Havel, from Mary Robinson to Bill Clinton, community was the new theme.

This theme had never been abandoned by Fitzmaurice; and in returning to it the world was learning once again that localism, far from being backward, is the very sign and shape of all our futures. Because of his deep understanding of Irish literary tradition, Fitzmaurice has never strayed from his *genius loci*. It might be predictable to cite at this point Kavanagh's cheerful parochialism as exemplary, or even Máirtín Ó Cadhain's *'caint leathpharáiste, caint leathurláir'*, but to be truthful, even their fidelity to their own places was that of a displaced person, an exile's tribute, a vivid recollection. The same might also be said of many other celebrants of a home territory from Máirtín Ó Direáin through Edna O'Brien to Seamus Heaney: for even though the townlands of Aran, Clare or South Derry are now unimaginable without their lyric evocations of them, it remains a fact that none of these writers was able to live on in the places so powerfully described. Fitzmaurice has been unusual in insisting (I think it is the proper word) on staying put. In a world where everything and everybody has been changing, this has been a near-revolutionary option, a truly audacious form of nesting. It has also been, in its own way, a kind of exile — exile from the more modish, obvious modes of audibility and visibility. To write stubbornly about a rural society at a time when the pundits and producers repeatedly quoted Karl Marx on 'the idiocy of rural life' took some courage, especially when the agenda embraced by the poet constituted a denial of the root-meaning of the word idiot — for 'a private person' is precisely what Fitzmaurice (or any of his characters) is not. To find a more useful analogy (without implying an equivalence of artistic achievement) one could consider the case of William Faulkner, defiantly rejecting the pay-checks of Hollywood and living out his days in Oxford, Mississippi, a place where the contours of art and reality exactly overlapped.

Faulkner, for all that *pietas*, turned out to be the modernist to end all modernists: and that is proof enough that the act of recording life in a deeply traditional community as it undergoes the catastrophic onset of modernity is itself labour enough for even the most versatile and probing of artists. So, also, with Fitzmaurice. Though he invokes the traditions of wren-boys, card-players, pub-singers, old-IRA men, or local characters, he does so in an accent that is anything but sentimental. His subjects are not locked into some folk museum but are dynamic participants who understand the revolutionary nature of tradition — that it is all about handing-on, crossing-over, adjusting without compromise to the demands of a global world. This may well be Fitzmaurice's innermost theme: for, sometimes, in his darker moments, he finds only in the past experience of his rural community that very terror which led him in some desperation to invoke it. He is unflinchingly honest about the soul-scarring violence as well as the fabled glamour of the revolutionary generation of the War of Independence.

In a similar way, he is candid about the weaknesses and emptinesses of today's community, which doesn't always live up to the pressure of his high hopes for it. At times, indeed, one senses that certain poems might be intended as much to define and promote the communitarian vision as to report it. If Kate O'Brien found that in recording the culture of a Catholic middle class, she had sometimes to invent aspects of a world she intended only to record, the same may be said of Fitzmaurice's poignant images of a rural community in transition, where the Sacred Heart lamp has been replaced by the cathode-tube of the TV set and the pattern-day by an outing to McDonald's.

Fitzmaurice hasn't set his face against TV or McDonald's: he has himself been a shrewd manipulator of the electronic media and is far too interested in modernity to be anything other than its fascinated chronicler. His real interest, however, is in transition, the moment when people pass over. He wants to know how tradition gets translated (if that isn't a tautology), so that the past is refined rather than rejected, developed rather than destroyed. Again, at a time when every second autobiography published seems to include a corrosive hostility to the recent past (than which nothing seems more remote or demeaning), that too is revolutionary.

Hence his concern to honour the patriots of an earlier time in an Ireland that was worriedly turning its back on them; the fact that he could honour their bravery, while questioning its continuing relevance, showed that a middle way might yet be found between adoration and amnesia. This poetry is a literal re-member-ing, a piecing-together of past and present moments which too often in the experience of other Irish communities have been condemned to separation, to dis-member-ing, and loss. This is the reason for Fitzmaurice's obsession with rural technicians and trades, like that of the thatcher — for the thatcher bound more than straw together.

It is also the real explanation for Fitzmaurice's wonderfully vivid poems of childhood: for at the core of his project is an insistence that nothing be lost, that the things of youth are never to be put away, since the artist is one who carries the feelings of childhood into the powers of the adult life. Reading some of the hilariously direct lyrics of his 'The Moving Stair' to my own children some years back, I was reminded of what Picasso once said to a critic who complained that a child could have produced some of his paintings. 'Yes,' he laughed gently, 'but could a child of forty have done them?' The continuing preoccupation with translations from the Irish in Fitzmaurice's work seems but another aspect of this demand that the past still breathe its energies into the present, that value can be added rather than lost with every generational transition, and that the real genius of Irish culture is its talent for adaptation.

There is in this volume a versatility of mind and imagination, a scope of experience and language, and an unusual generosity of spirit. Fitzmaurice seeks cultural enfranchisement for the dead as well as the living, for the child as well as the pensioner. Through him a whole community enters dialogue with itself: and even as the poet speaks through his chosen words, the language itself realises its genius through him. It is hardly necessary to add that his is a voice which also carries inflections of American, English, Gaelic and European poetry. In getting to the roots of his own place, he has come to terms with the world.

The bargain struck between tradition and the individual talent is in this case a fair one. And the proof is that the world is beginning to notice and approve the kind of poetry which suggests that the community, far from being a confederacy of dunces raised in militant mediocrity against the individual, is the place where best the individual can grow and flourish.

Declan Kiberd

dinnsheanchas: (Irish) the lore of place
caint leathpharáiste, caint leathurláir: (Irish) the talk of half a parish, the talk of half a floor

Lovers

Is it the clothes
Or is it the socks?
There's a sweet smell of dirt off me.
I smell of my friends —
Must take a wash.

A lunatic laughs at Mass
(It's really a sin,
But to be normal
Is to laugh at him).

He laughs at us —
At our cleanliness,
At our fuss.
Better to go and hustle
Like him.

Your car was wrecked,
You buy one new —
Who hasn't a ha'penny
Well God bless you.

The river,
Convulsed like a lunatic
Stormed on a table,
Is called Annamoy.
I love it
Because it's a hopeless river.
But sun, clouds, cows
Quiver in it,
Wagtails ripple over it,
While bulls trample its stones.

The village is Newtown Sandes
Called Moyvane ('The Middle Plain')
For hate of landlords.
New people don't like it.
I want to die in it.

Like the mad
Flirting with the happy and sad
And hope and the rope
And water,
The people like islanders
Await the disaster
And live.
Dogs and simpletons
Plough the midday swirl of dust and papers.

I did a line with the city,
Made love to a town,
But always that dung-sotted river
Leafed me home.

Newtown, you bastard,
You'll break me, I know:
New women won't live here,
Our women have left here
And always I grow old.

Like a dog and its master,
Like a ship on the water,
I need you, you bitch,
Newtown.

I need you, you bitch,
Newtown.

Derelicts

Whenever I picture the village fools
They drool with the hump
Of benevolence on their backs.
Living in hovels as I remember,
They had the health of the rat.

They perched on the street-corner
Like crows around the carcass
Of a lamb. Stale bread and sausages
Would feed a hungry man.
Beady with the cunning of survival,
Each pecked the other from his carrion.

Children feared them like rats in a sewer—
They stoned their cabins
And the stones lay at the door.

Like priests, they were the expected,
The necessary contrary —
We bow in gratitude for mediocre lives;
We keep the crow, the rat from the garden.
Like priests, no one mourned when they died.

When they died, we pulled down their cabins;
Then we transported a lawn
That the mad, the hopeless might be buried—
Only the strong resisting (while strong).
We kept the grass and flowerbeds neatly
But the wilderness wouldn't be put down.

Children no longer play there
(They stone it),
Nettles stalk the wild grass,
Scutch binds the stones together...

Then came the rats.

Hay

for
my father

1

Heavy bales are hoors.
The shed is no place
If you're not too strong.
Sweat sticks
Like hay to wool
And the rhythm of hay
Is the last native dance.

Will it ever stop,
This suicidal monotone of hay?
It goes on like a depression
In the rural brain.

Hay
(Long ago the days were longer)

Hay
(Long ago the men were stronger)

Hay
(Long ago you gave a day's labour
For a day's pay)
(It didn't rain in Summer long ago)

Hay Hay Hay

2

I bought a bulk milk container,
I built another shed —
Everyone advised me that

The ass-and-cart, the tank
Were dead.

My father would surely wonder now
At the size of my great herd.

I've bulldozed uneconomic ditches
That made *Garraí Beag, Fearann, Móinéar* —
This great new field I'm fencing
Has no name.

My father
Spoke to his cows in Winter
In the stall.
Connor knew his herd by name —
He fed them on *the long acre*
And was put in jail.

There was a priest here once
Who ranted that a man
Measured his importance
In the size of his dung-hill,
The poor clout!

Nowadays
You measure your importance
In the size of your bulk container.
Shortly they'll open
'The Club of the Bulk Container:
Farmers Not Allowed'.

The good is modern —
You can't opt out.

3

Once I made wynds
In small meadows for fear of rain.
Some of the hay was green.
A friendly dog kept jumping on my back.
We had time for a fag
And porter at the gap.

Later
We milked the cows by hand
And strained the milk with a rag—
'A white cloth', we called it.

We laughed in those days
We did
We did

We laughed...

Garraí Beag: (Irish) The Small Garden (pronounce *Gorry Be-ug*)
Fearann: (Irish) A Field, Ploughland (pronounce *Farran*)
Móinéar: (Irish) A Meadow (pronounce *Mow-nare*)
The long acre: (dialect) The grass margin at the side of the road

Epitaph

A colossus on the playing field,
A great man for *the crack*,
For years he spoke to no-one
But turned his sagging back on people;
Head down, he would cycle into town.

Whispers prodded that he be seen to—
'Looked after,' slyly said.
Anyone could see
That his head was out of joint.
And he couldn't even hold his lonely pint.

They found him hanging in the barn, dead.
Viciousness turned almost to understanding—
Living alone, never wed,
'His uncle did it years before him.
Kind for him,' they said.

The crack: (dialect) fun, high jinks
Kind for him: (dialect) It was in his nature, in his family

The Skald Crow

for
John Moriarty

At first I didn't know you —
You were a stranger when you came;
I fed you in winter,
I nursed you when you were lame.

You screwed your black beak
Into my brain —
You fed yourself when you were hungry;
I croaked your song.

You are stronger than hope,
Stronger than despair,
Stronger than love,
You are stronger than hate.

Against you I have no litany
But to call you me,
And though you'd trick me
Into felling the tree you nest on,
I'll not cut down the tree.

In the beginning, you came to me.

Garden

for
Brenda

We were a garden dug by eager hands;
Weeds were swept by shovels underground;
Brown earth, blackened and split by Winter,
Was picked to a skeleton by starving birds.

Spring surprised us with a yelp of daisies
Defiant as a terrier guarding his home ground;
We planted seed in the cleft of drills
Slimy with earthworms.

Today I picked the first fruit of our garden—
Bloody with earth, I offered it to you;
You washed it and anointed it,
We ate it like viaticum.

In the eating of pith and seed
I loved you.

Poem for Brenda

I

The White Page

1

With love inarticulate as the draft
Revised
Despaired of

Revised
Crossed

Lover to lover cannot say
His deepest words.

And the white page beckons
Like a poacher's light
And words break cover
As the fight begins
On the periphery of sense
Where meaning lingers
And word ends.

2

Then silence.
The battle over.

We return to decipher in this spent rage
The voices that were voiceless
Of the words we twisted shapeless,

To lay out the carnage
On the marble of the page

Till sound and sense agree

Redeemed in this arrangement,
This obituary.

II

A Language

'Lover to lover cannot say
His deepest words'
Are my words
And half true.

But love finds the voices
That lurk behind the clichés.

Now words regress
To repossess some vast, sunny Eden of youth
Where a child can tell his child lover
A childish truth
And games of love and hate
Are created articulate.

Now the sap is rising
Thick as dew —

In or out of this garden
I can never lie to you
Though a language compromises truth.

III

Another Language

With you
I am husband,

Singer,
Poet
Forever sounding words for truth.

I edge beyond the edges of my depth
Returning always safely
(Next time to be swept?) —
The road to the horizon has no end.

There are times when you call words from me like sperm.

And together we have sounded the pristine words
Until our mouths together are one tongue
And sense has woken to its language
And all the nameless impulses of brain
Flow towards understanding.

And I salute you, Brenda with 'Brenda hello'
Where our native tongue would bless you
And so
Because we know the silent understanding
I bring new words to you, Brenda,
Once again.

A Game of Forty-One

Tonight it's forty-one:
Pay to your right, 10p a man.
Doubles a jink, and play your hand.
If you renege, we'll turn you.

Yes, tonight it's forty-one:
A table for six, any pub in town.
Follow suit, and stand your round.
If you renege, we'll turn you.

Tonight it's forty-one
And tomorrow in the Dáil
Fine Gael and Fianna Fáil
Debate their Bill —

'Cos on the television
They're talking of revision
And extension of detention
And extra Special Powers.

So we sit here hour by hour
Getting drunk on special Power:
A game of cards at night now
Costs more and more and more.

And you trump hard on the table,
And you pay up when you're able.
If you don't, then you're in trouble —
It's worse than to renege.

Oh, it's always forty-one:
Play your cards at work, at home —

Even sitting on a barstool
They won't let you alone.

Yes, it's always forty-one,
And I'm really in the dumps
For the horsemouth at my elbow
Has just led the Ace of Trumps.

And I'm playing forty-one
And wishing there were some
Other way of spending
A lifetime in this town.

But the poet and the priest
— Beauty and the Beast —
Must all sit down together
And cut this common deck.

And there is no Bill or Bible
But the verdict of the table
And the argument of players
To dispute the point of rule.

So tonight it's forty-one
And tomorrow, next week, next month,
And I'm out if I suggest
Another rule.

We'll turn you: (dialect) We'll put you out of this round of cards
Dáil: (Irish) Parliament of the Irish Republic (pronounce *Dawl*)
Fine Gael and Fianna Fáil: The two largest political parties in the Irish
    Republic

Stripping a Chair

for
Desmond Egan

Gloss dissolves
Then wrinkles.

Layers peel
To the first bonding
Of paint and wood.

The knife cuts
Through generations
Of enhancement

Till further stripping
Damages the wood.

Grit reaches
To the residue
Of the first painting

As the first crude vision
Is sanded smooth.

This was the true vision.

Who made this chair was no craftsman
Of curve and mortise —

This chair served its purpose
And didn't interrupt
The daily drudge.

The Hurt Bird

After playtime
Huddled in the classroom...

In the yard
Jackdaws peck the ice
While the class guesses
The black birds:

Blackbirds?
(Laughter).

Crows?
Well yes...
But jackdaws.
Those are jackdaws.
Why do they peck the ice?

Wonder
Becomes jackdaws' eyes
Rummaging the ice

Till suddenly
At the window opposite

— Oh the bird!
The poor bird!

At the shout
The jackdaws fright.

Sir, a robin sir...
He struck the window

And he fell
And now he's dying
With his legs up
On the ice:

The jackdaws
Will attack it sir,

They will rip its puddings out.

I take the wounded bird,
Deadweight
In my open palm

— No flutter
No escaping

And lay it on the floor near heat,
The deadweight
Of the wound
Upon my coat.

Grasping
The ways of pain,
The pain of birds
They cannot name,
The class are curious
But quiet:

They will not frighten
The struggle
Of death and living.

Please sir,
Will he die?

And I
Cannot reply.

Alone
With utter pain

Eyes closed

The little body
Puffed and gasping

Lopsided
Yet upright:

He's alive,
The children whisper
Excited
As if witnessing
His birth.

Would he drink water sir?
Would he eat bread?
Should we feed him?

Lopsided
The hurt bird
With one eye open
To the world
Shits;

He moves
And stumbles.
I move
To the hurt bird:

The beak opens

— For food
Or fight?

I touch
The puffed red breast
With trepid finger;

I spoon water
To the throat:

It splutters.

Children crumb their lunches
Pleading to lay the broken bread
Within reach of the black head.

The bird
Too hurt to feed
Falls in the valley
Of the coat,
And as I help
It claws
And perches on my finger
Bridging the great divide
Of man and bird.

He hops
From my finger
To the floor
And flutters
Under tables
Under chairs

Till exhausted
He tucks his head

Between wing and breast
Private
Between coat and wall.

The class
Delights in silence
At the sleeping bird.

The bird sir...
What is it —
A robin?
— Look at the red breast.

But you never see a robin
With a black head.

I tell them
It's a bullfinch
Explaining the colours why:

I answer their questions
From the library.

And the children draw the bullfinch

— With hurt
And gasp
And life

With the fearlessness of pain
Where the bird will fright

And in the children's pictures
Even black and grey
Are bright.

Hunting the Wren

> The Wren, the Wren, the king of all birds,
> Saint Stephen's Day he was caught in the furze
> So up with the kettle and down with the pan
> And give us a penny to bury the Wren.
>
> *Traditional Rhyme*

The villages of Ireland have lost their tongue
And ritual descends to custom
For custom to become some conservation,
Some parody of the spirit.

The romp of spirit, the riot of soul
Is pathetic when ritual lacks a rôle.
And so, the Christmas over, we hunt the Wren
But the hunt assumes no meaning.

We are the flower of that which died before us
And if we do not know what died, or why it died,
We walk in darkness.

Who would hunt the Wren must first let darkness in.
We will have inherited our ancestry
If the symbol is within.

Symbol of a mystic people is the Wren
On the march of the imagination.

So let us go in darkest Winter to hunt the Wren
With skin of goat that was sacrificed for a drum,
With the Wren totem on the holly bush.
Masked, let all the village come
With rattle of bones and hoofbeat of *bodhrán*,

With music to charm the spirit of the Wren,
With dancing to express the form of music,
With the archaic pageant ordered in a song
For this is the truth of Wrenboys
And we must pass it on
In the carnival of darkness,
Singers of the sun.

Bodhrán: A traditional goatskin drum (pronounce *bow-rawn*)

Keeper

for
my father

First
My father mowing —
Turning an early spring
Into a green lawn.

And again
A sun of daisy and dandelion —

My father mows the lawn.

Then
My father weeding
Daisy and dandelion,
Patient fingers
Perennial with white slime —

My father:
Keeper of his lawn,
His mind.

The Poet's Garden

There's a pollen of bees
In the heart of the flowers

A survival of grubs
In the cabbage

A compost of words
At one end of the plot

At the other
A stillbirth of garbage

Predator

for
Vincent Buckley

Within the woods, the coolness of the sea.
The lesser birds and songbirds all have fled.
Fern, dock and nettle bend before me,
But I have lost the ancient lore of herbs.

The undergrowth is barbed, a fence of brambles,
And I have come to feed on wilderness;
Like fur, these bits of human where I stumbled
Are tugged by rooks and jackdaws for their nests.

Bleakness of woods dying under ivy —
Here a tree, moss-splintered, home of lice;
Here a branch whose shoots have burst, divided
From lichened bark: bud-red grows branchlet-bright.

As if the crows could turn away the stranger,
They wheel their frantic chainsaw-song of fright.
Crows in the crow dominion sense the danger:
The flightless beast looks up, protects his eyes.

The Spider and the Fly

for
D.J. Enright

Won't you come into my parlour,
Says the spider to the fly.
You can't deny me:
Effort is useless against me.

I am anarchic as imagination
And treacherous as sex;
I am stronger than your will.
Come into my parlour.

Here slave is master,
Master slave.
In this parlour
Is all you crave.
Here wounds open
That were healed:
Here all secrets
Are revealed.
Come into my parlour.

You strain against me
But I own your brain.
You should have learned
That I possess you.
Again and again
You pull against me
To no avail.
Try as you will to root me out
You'll fail.

Regale me.

Sing: *Hail spider!*
Hail! All hail!
The spider is all-powerful
Where you are frail.

Come into my parlour,
Says the spider to the fly.
Do not deny your nature.
Accept that you're a creature
Subservient to me.

Accept
And fly and spider
Will agree
For the spider is in you
As the fly is part of me.

                *

I am spider
I am fly —
That much I can't deny

And I have tried
To maintain that great divide

But why?

If the spider and the fly
Are one already,
I must open up my parlour.

Oh fly that lacks a spider
Oh spider that lacks a fly
Come into my parlour

— Softly I.

Virgin Rock, Ballybunion

for
Johnny Coolahan

Surrounded by breakers
I stand
Where the grinding ocean
Turns weakness into sand.
I approach my true shape,
Being weathered —
Cliff to rock to strand...

In the Midst of Possibility

Now I love you
Free of me:
In this loving I can see
The *You* of you
Apart from me —
The *You* of you that's ever free.

This is the *You* I love.
This is the *You* I'll never have.
This is the *You* beyond possession —

The *You* that's ever true
While ever changing,
Ever new.

Now,
Naked,
Free,
The *You* of you
Meets the *Me* of me
And to see is to love,
To love, to see:

In the midst of possibility
We agree.

The Pregnant Earth

for
Gyozo Ferencz

The hurt was there before me,
Inherent in my genes;

The hurt was all around me
And I heard;

The hurt drove one to suicide,
Stripped another's nerves,
And turned one to singing.

＊

And I became a singer —
My songs flew wild and free,
But the hurt's gravity tethered them
As it had tethered me.

And I became a cave-man
Groping in my soul,
Hacking at obstruction
For light to fill the hole
Till my eyes became bats' eyes
And I found my way through echoes
In the dark.

＊

The pregnant earth,
Midwinter,
Sings its song to me,
Humming in its belly:

Arise, Persephone...

This simple song sustains me
As the darkness claims its dead —

O light within the darkness,
O carol in my head...

Getting to Know You

Thomas,
You don't trust me —
I can tell from your trapped eyes.
How can I help you,
My sulky friend?
Tell you I love you?
(That would seem like lies).
To reach out to touch you
Might offend.

Give you your head;
Watch over
In so far as any human can;
Coax you with tacit kindness;
Greet you, man to man...

Yes, Thomas,
I am strong
(But equal) —
And, Thomas,
We are both 'at school':
Both circling round
A common understanding,
Both sniffing at the smile
That sweetens rules.

Today you bounce up to me,
Your eyes the rising sun:

We share your secret story —

Hello!
God bless you,
Tom...

Dancing Through

Homage to
Mikey Sheehy, footballer

Nureyev with a football,
You solo to the goal
Where the swell of expectation
Spurts in vain —
O master of the ritual,
O flesh of tribal soul,
Let beauty be at last
Released from pain...

Now grace eludes its marker
Creating its own space
While grim defenders
Flounder in its wake;
And the ball you won from conflict
Yields to your embrace —
Goal beckons like a promise...
And you take.

Presentation

On Christmas Eve
We present our child
(Adopted after all these years)
First
In the ancestral home.

Tom, *paterfamilias*,
Kisses him.

This is the floor
Tom's father crawled,
My father crawled.

Mary,
Woman of the house,
Coaxes him across the floor.

Now
You're a Fitzmaurice

And in this ancestral home
With cousins,
Aunts and uncles
You are welcome;

For you're our new communion—
The family receive
As Mary pours a health to you
On this first Christmas Eve.

Ties

'Son'
I call you
And the name possesses:

What the Board made legal,
The word makes true.

Your first 'da-da',
My first 'son'
Have named our recognition.

Later
You may venture on your own,
Seeking
What even this love can't give.

No matter:

We inhabit our appellations,
'Daddy'
'Son',
Part of each other's language...

This will live.

Art

You sprawl on the floor
Scribbling on an invoice
Ignoring *Tom and Jerry* on TV.

'I make it! I write the picture!',
You divert me, imploring
'That's John's picture'.

I let you be.

Then
'Up Daybo's lap!',
You dance and tug me.

'No John!
Daybo's writing poems' —

A pause...

'John write a pone! John write a pone!',
You barter.

Your ploy shines on refusal
And it thaws.

Sitting on my lap
You grab my biro,
Cover Daybo's draft about you
With your scrawl —

'That's Daybo's pone', you beam,
'Dirty! Dirty!'

Inherent in creation is its fall.

Beebla

for
John and Nessa

Beebla wasn't sure that he was born
(What was it to be born? He didn't know),
But his mother had been dying four or five times:
Beebla threatened God: 'Don't let her go —
If You do, then I won't say my prayers;
If You do, then I won't go to Mass.'
The priest came and anointed Beebla's Mammy.
Next morning, Beebla boasted in his class:
'My mother was anointed in the night-time;
The priest came to our house, I stayed up late.'
Beebla was cock-proud of his achievement:
All the class was listening — this was great!

Beebla played with all the boys at playtime
(The girls were in the school across the way) —
They played football with a sock stuffed with old papers,
He'd forget about his Mammy in the play.
But always at the back of all his playing,
He knew about anointing in the night,
And, knowing this, there could be no un-knowing —
Nothing in the world would change that quite.

Beebla got a motor-car in London —
A blue one with pedals which he craved
(Beebla'd been in hospital in London,
And, coming home, he'd had to have his way);
So his Daddy bought him his blue motor-car,
He drove it all the way out to the 'plane,
And touching down, cranky with excitement,
He squealed till he was in his car again.

He drove around the village, a born show-off;
He pulled into a funeral, kept his place,
And all the funeral cars, backed up behind him,
Couldn't hoot, for that would be disgrace!
He drove off from the Chapel to the graveyard,
And, tiring, he pulled out and headed back;
When his mother heard about it, she went purple
And grabbed for her *wallop-spoon* to smack;

But his Daddy shielded Beebla from her wallops—
They brushed across his Daddy's legs until
His mother's rage fizzled to a token:
She shook the spoon, and threatened that she'd kill
Him if he didn't mind his manners:
But Beebla went on driving, till one day
A real car almost hit him at the Corner:
For safety, they took his car away.
Beebla didn't cry or throw a tantrum—
He knew that but for luck he would be dead,
And at night-time, after kisses, hugs and lights-out,
He started up his car inside his head.

Beebla got a piano once from Santa—
He ran down to the Church on Christmas Day
Before his Mammy or his Daddy could contain him
(He wanted all the crowd to hear him play).
And he walloped notes and pounded them and thumped them
As 'Silent Night' became a noisy day,
But it was *his* noise, all his own and he could make it—
It said things for him that only it could say.

And he stole into the Church another morning
When all the crowd had scattered home from Mass,
And he went up to the *mike* like Elvis Presley
But he only made an echo — it was off!

So Beebla went back home to his piano,
To the sound of what it is to be alone
'Cos Beebla had no brothers or no sisters
And he often had to play all on his own.

Beebla was the crossest in the village —
He was not afraid of beast or man:
He'd jump off walls, climb trees, walk under horses —
He did it for a dare; until the Wren
When the Wren Boys dressed up in masks and sashes
And came into your house to dance and play —
Beebla was excited at the Wren Boys,
He simply couldn't wait for Stephen's Day;
But when the Wren Boys came to Beebla's kitchen
Like horrors that he dreaded in his dreams,
He howled, tore off into the bathroom,
And hid behind the bath and kicked and screamed.

His mother came and told him not to worry,
Brought Tom Mangan into him without the mask —
Tom Mangan was his friend, worked in the Creamery,
But today Tom Mangan caused his little heart
To pound inside his ribcage like a nightmare,
Was fear dressed up and playing for hard cash —
Tom would be his friend again tomorrow,
But today Beebla hung around the bath.

He ran away from school the day he started —
He ran before he got inside the door
And his friends who'd brought him there that morning
Couldn't catch him. But he'd no time to explore
The village that morning in December
Before Christmas trees were common, or lights lit —
Beebla had to figure out his problem
And he wasn't sure how he'd get out of it.

He stole into his shop and no-one noticed
(His Daddy's shop — his Mammy wasn't well)
And he hid beneath the counter till Daddy found him:
'Oh Daddy, Daddy, Daddy, please don't tell
Mammy that I ran from school this morning—
The doors were big and dark, the windows high;
And Dad, I ran from school this morning
— I had to — 'twas either that or cry'.
His Daddy didn't mind, his Mammy neither,
He stayed at home till Eastertime, and then
One morning he got dressed-up, took his schoolbag,
Brushed his hair, and went to school again.

He played with all the boys in *The Back Haggarts*,
A place that has no name (it's gone!) today,
High jumps, long jumps, triple jumps and marbles,
But there was one game not everyone could play—
The secret game that he was once allowed in:
'Doctors' where you pulled down your pants
To be examined by one who was 'The Doctor';
Beebla ran when asked to drop his pants!
And they chased him, calling him 'a coward',
But Beebla didn't want to play that fun
(Mostly 'cos a girl was 'The Doctor')
He ran in home but didn't tell anyone.

And one time, too, he fought a boy for nothing
'Cos the older boys had goaded them to fight;
After that, he never fought for nothing
'Cos he knew inside himself it wasn't right.

Beebla would annoy you with his questions—
He wanted to know everything — and why:
Why he was, what was it to be Beebla,
And would his mother live, or would she die?

And what was it to die? Was it like *Cowboys*
Where you could live and die and live again?
Or would Mammy be forever up in Heaven?
(Forever was how much times one-to-ten?)

This was all before the television,
About the time we got electric light,
Before bungalows, bidets or flush-toilets,
Where dark was dark, and fairies roamed the night.
This story's a true story — *honest Injun*!
You tell me that it's funny, a bit sad;
Be happy! It has a happy ending
'Cos Beebla grew up to be your Dad.

Galvin and Vicars

in memoriam Mick Galvin, killed in action, Kilmorna, Knockanure
(in the parish of Newtown Sandes, now Moyvane) on Thursday,
7 April 1921;

Sir Arthur Vicars, shot at Kilmorna House, his residence, on
Thursday, 14 April 1921.

Mick Galvin, Republican,
Arthur Vicars, who knows what?
— Some sort of Loyalist —
In Ireland's name were shot:

Vicars by Republicans,
Galvin by the Tans,
Both part of my history —
The parish of Newtown Sandes

Named to flatter landlords
(But 'Moyvane' today,
Though some still call it 'Newtown' —
Some things don't go away

Easily). Galvin and Vicars,
I imagine you as one —
Obverse and reverse
Sundered by the gun.

History demands
We admit each other's wrongs:
Galvin and Vicars,
Joined only in this song,

Nonetheless I join you
In the freedom of this state
For art discovers symmetries
Where politics must wait.

Tans: i.e. *Black and Tans*, a unit of the Crown forces during the Irish War
of Independence

Two Brothers

Two brothers joined the Column
To fight for Ireland Free,
Then the Treaty divided them;
The story that united
Shattered with the dream:
A man without a story
Is a man who must redeem himself.
The community of purpose
Shattered like a glass,
Each seeing his own image
Singly, piece by piece
Where once all life was mirrored;
He would again be whole —
Fighting for their stories,
Comrades, brothers, soldiers
Join in Civil War
And so did these two brothers.
They never again shared
Sleep beneath the same roof,
A pint in any bar,
Dinner at one table.
And so, the fighting over,
They both moved to the Bronx,
Married, raised families —
Never once
Did they communicate.
I remember as a child
Their (separate) Summer visits,
Two storied men who smiled at me
And played my childish games:
I remember with affection,
At times recite their names

When opposite is opposite.
Some things won't unite:
Wounds will knit, not stories
Till the poetry is right.

Column: i.e. Flying Column, an active service unit of the IRA during the
War of Independence.

Survivor

Captain, I remember you
Praying every day
At the statue of Saint Anthony
For the men you shot. They

Haunted you in your old age
To your asylum — prayer:
This faith that once divided you,
That fought a Civil War

To forge order from division,
Sustained you, though the state
That both sides fought for
Neither could create;

But, for all that, a Republic
Where you played the Captain's part
Biting every bullet,
Knowing in your heart

That, though the war is over
And we vote in liberty,
There's a *Britain* in all of us
From which we're never free.

Among the Nations

to the memory of
my grand-uncle, Mick Foran ('Stanley')

'...Let no man write my epitaph; for as no man
who knows my motives dares now vindicate them,
let not prejudice or ignorance asperse them. Let
them and me rest in obscurity and peace, and my
tomb remain uninscribed, and my memory in
oblivion, until other times and other men can do
justice to my character. When my country takes
her place among the nations of the earth, then, and
not till then, let my epitaph be written.'
> from Robert Emmet's *Speech from the Dock*
> 19 September, 1803

Stanley, I feel I know you,
Contrairy to the end —
A public entertainment,
A soul without a friend;

An accidental patriot
— Jailed in Ireland's cause
For singing 'seditious ballads'
Contrary to law.

You shrugged off opportunity,
Shunned the hero's name—
The perks it would have brought you,
You didn't care to claim;

For what was Independence?
— A fabulous regime,
Yet a state you could have sung against
And still be no shoneen.

Freedom is a state of mind
That none can plot or graph —
Uncle, devil's advocate,
This is your epitaph.

Contrairy: Hiberno-English roughly corresponding to the English
'contrary' — cross, perverse, cranky, crotchety
Shoneen: (Hiberno-English) contemptuously refers to an Irish person
aping English ways; there is a hint of betrayal in the word

The Common Touch

for
Robert McDowell

Perky Nolan was a stuck-up dog —
The schoolmaster's.
He never fought with the other dogs that held the street.
He was manicured as street-urchins would never be.

Perky went for *walkies* with the master's daughter,
Manicured as herself.
Beside her, Perky tiptoed like a dancer;
He cocked his leg, important as the Anthem in Croke Park;
He cocked his nose, a mammy's boy,
And broadcast with his bark.

Perky was all the things a villager would never be,
And so the village waited.

One day Perky got loose and walked free;
The village nosed him.
Perky made a show of baring teeth,
But there was no harm in him.

This was the chance we'd waited for.

'Perky! Here boy! Here boy!
Good dog! Good dog!'
We called, holding out our hands.
Perky sniffed and padded towards us.

'Kick the shit out of him boys,' we exploded.
Shoes, boots, wellingtons and bare toes thudded into him.
He howled and ran.

'That'll teach him to put on airs,' the village gloated.

Perky found the common touch —
The same for dog and man.

Ode to a Bluebottle

It never is quite summer
Till you fizz around the room,
Drone to summer's chanter,
Spurt, a loosed balloon.

It never is quite summer
Till you're splattered on the sill:
Oh, we don't want all of summer.
Much of it we kill.

Willie Dore

Willie Dore was simple,
He smelled. The village fool,
He lived alone among the rats
In a shack below the school.

Two rats' eyes in his leather face
Stabbed out beneath the layer
Of dirt that blackened him like soot.
He wasn't born *quare*,

But some disease the doctor
Couldn't cure (or name)
Trapped him in his childhood
Hobbling his brain.

Willie Dore was a happy man
Though peevish as a huff —
He fed, he drank, he slept, he rose,
He dreamed — that was enough...

Each sausage scrounged from a travelling van
Was a vital victory;
Each penny coaxed from a passing priest
Was a cunning comedy.

Willie never knew his age —
No matter how you'd pry,
'The one age to Mary Mack'
Was all he could reply.

He lived as he imagined,
Saw manna in the street,
Eighty years of scavenging,
Admitting no defeat.

Quare: (dialect) a version of 'queer' meaning 'strange', 'unusual', 'mentally unbalanced'

The Village Hall

The old Hall with its shaky stage
Was good enough for us —
Bill Horan and Eileen Manaher
Wholly marvellous

As they called up here before us
A world of their own,
The magic I have grown to love,
The farce I loved, outgrown.

The queue outside the musty Hall,
The key turned in the lock,
The stampede to the benches,
The fizz, the sweets, clove rock;

And then the silence as the play
Took us in its spell,
Local folk turned Gods and Queens
In this miracle.

The Hall is old, not worth repair,
They'll knock it, build anew;
My boy and girl will taste in there
The magic that I knew;

They'll find the things a village finds
In the local Hall —
That as Eileen becomes a Queen
We're not ourselves at all.

'I Thirst'

Midnight Mass one Christmas Eve,
The Parish comes to pray —
A midnight of nostalgia
After a hard day;

For some have been preparing
Their Christmas at the sink,
And others have spent the day
Revelling in drink.

At Midnight Mass, the Parish
Bows its head in prayer —
All but one have come along
In pious posture there.

All day, he's been drinking
In The Corner House;
When it comes to closing time
He buys, to carry out
For after Mass, two bottles
Of Guinness Extra Stout.

And he stands there with the others
At the back wall of the Church;
When it comes to the Offertory,
Suddenly with a lurch

He staggers up the centre aisle
While the crowd looks on in shock,
Halting at the altar rails,
Careful not to drop

The bottles, he takes them out,
Plants them on the rails,
Faces the congregation,
Waves and then repairs

To the back and anonymity,
Hitches up his arse,
And some are shocked, and some amused
At this unholy farce.

But the Christ who thirsts on Calvary
Has waited all these years
For a fellow cursed with the cross of thirst
To stand him these few beers.

Good Friday

Good Friday was the day of periwinkles:
The only day we got them — oh the treat!
An old lady and her son came up from Bally
With an assload. They were much more fun than meat.

They sold them by the handful to us children;
We took them home and pestered Mom for pins.
They looked like snots when you fished them out. But Jesus!
That was some way to atone for all your sins!

We ate them by the fistful all that morning,
Receiving the essence of the tide.
The empty shells prefigured eggs for Easter.
At three o'clock the Christ was crucified.

The tang of winkles flavours my Good Fridays,
The emptiness familiar as the day.
The old woman's dead, her son too. Every weekend
The winkle man revives them on his tray.

In Memoriam Danny Cunningham 1912–1995

I take her to the Funeral Home —
She wants to see him dead;
She's not afraid — she rubs his hands
And then explores his head.

'He not wake up I rub him.
Look Daddy! He not move.
Where Danny, Dad?' she asks me.
'*Danny's dead, my love*'.

'Where Danny, Dad', she asks again;
Then suddenly it's clear —
'The old Danny in the box', she says;
'The new one — he not here'.

Oisín's Farewell to Niamh

No-one can live forever
And even if we could
We'd choose death in the long run.
This is good.

Tír na nÓg's for children —
Nothing changes there,
Everyone always smiling,
Flowers in their hair;

And all their songs are child's songs
Where nothing ever grows,
But to a poet and soldier,
To such a one as knows

The death-and-birth of seasons,
Though Eternal Youth's his bride,
Such a one must live his life,
Such a one can't hide

In eternal youth and happiness
Where nothing ever dies —
Once you've lived with mortals
Tír na nÓg is lies.

So fare thee well, my Princess,
I must leave you now, my dear,
Back to death in Ireland
To face my fear.

Tír na nÓg: (Irish) Land of Eternal Youth (pronounce *Teer na Nogue*)

A Bedtime Story

I want to give my children what I got—
A sign of middle age and childhood past:
'A story about Daddy — tell us what
You did when you were little — just like us.'
What survives our childhood we don't choose—
We must forgive our childhood if we can:
We cannot cite our childhood as excuse—
Hurt is not a licence to do wrong.
And so I bring my children to my past,
A past that was unhappy as 'twas good—
A story now, and so my kids have guessed
The happy ending, as indeed they should.
I tuck them in as sleep tugs at their lids.
I hope they'll wish their childhood on their kids.

May Dalton

The last word that was left to her was 'honour',
The stroke had taken all the rest away,
The one thing the void could not take from her
Was herself, and so she used to say
'Honour! Honour! Honour!' when you addressed her,
'Honour! Honour! Honour!' while her hand
Clutched her agitation. What depressed her
Was how those closest failed to understand
'Honour! Honour! Honour!', how our beaming
Was the beaming of an adult at a child:
'Honour! Honour! Honour!' had no meaning
For any but May Dalton. So we smiled.
A single word held all she had to say;
Enclosed within this word, she passed away.

The Teacher

for
David Mason

I wish away my life until the pension
Hoping that, just once, I will connect
With sympathy that is beyond attention;
Instead I keep good order, earn respect.
Once I had a vision for my village —
I'd bring to it a gift of poetry;
Tonight the talk's of quotas and of tillage
And how the barmaid gives out beer for free.
And yet, I've not lost hope in my own people—
My vision was at fault; these people need
To sing and dance, get drunk below the steeple
That accuses them of gossip and of greed.
I mind their children, give them right of way
Into a world I've seen and try to say.

To Martin Hayes, Fiddler

All that we are given, we can use;
All the notes are there for us to praise—
The tune's set out before us, yet we choose:
The tune evolves in playing. Martin Hayes
Susses out each note before he cues
It. Taking thought, he chooses what it says,
Weaves into the fabric his own news:
The tune's predestined, not the way he plays.

The music *is*, the fiddler's taken thought—
All our moments lead to this last doh,
All the options, everything that's sought:
What we hear that's played is what we know.
Holy! Holy! Holy! what is wrought!
He raises up, rubs rosin to the bow.

The Yellow Bittern

Bitter, bird, it is to see
After all your spree, your bones stretched, dead;
Not hunger — No! by thirst laid low,
Flattened here on the back of your head.
It's worse than the ruin of Troy to me
To see you stretched among bare rock
Who never did harm nor treachery
Preferring water to finest hock.

My lovely bird, I sorely grieve
To see you stretched beside my path
Where you would swill and drink your fill
And from the puddle I'd hear your rasp.
Everyone warns your brother Cathal
That the drink will kill him, to stop and think;
But that's not so — observe this crow
Lately dead for want of drink.

My youthful bird, I'm so depressed
To see you stretched among the gorse
And the rats assembling for your waking
To sport and pleasure by your corpse.
And if you'd only sent a message
That you were in a fix, and dry,
I'd have split the ice upon Lake Vesey,
You'd have wet your mouth and your craw inside.

It's not for these birds that I'm mourning,
The blackbird, songthrush or the crane
But my yellow bittern, a hearty fellow,
Like me in colour, habit, name.
He was ever drinking, drinking

And so am I (they say I'm cursed)—
There's no drop I'm offered that I won't scoff
For fear that I might die of thirst.

'Give up the booze,' my darling begs me,
''Twill be your death.' Not so, I think;
I correct my dear's delusion—
I'll live longer the more I'll drink.
Look at this smooth-throated tippler
Dead from drought beside me here—
Good neighbours all, come wet your whistles
For in the grave you'll drink no beer.

from the Irish of Cathal Buí Mac Giolla Ghunna
(c. 1690–1756)

Cill Aodáin

Now Spring is upon us, the days will be stretching,
And after *The Biddy* I'll hoist up and go;
Since I've decided, there'll be no returning
Till I stand in the middle of County Mayo.
In the town of Claremorris I'll spend the first evening,
And in Balla below it the first drinks will flow,
Then to Kiltimagh travel to spend a whole month there
Barely two miles from Ballinamore.

I set down forever that my spirit rises
Like fog as it scatters, as wind starts to blow
When I'm thinking of Carra or Balla below it,
Or Scahaveela or the plain of Mayo.
Cill Aodáin the fertile, where all fruits are growing —
Blackberries, raspberries, full-fruited each one,
And if I were standing among my own people
The years they would leave me, again I'd be young.

from the Irish of Antoine Ó Reachtabhra (Raftery)
(c. 1784–1835)

The Biddy: Saint Brigid's Day, the first day of Spring
Cill Aodáin: the poet's place of birth (pronounce *Kill Ay-dawn*)

A Change

'Come over,' said Turnbull, 'and look at the sorrow
In the horse's eyes.
If you had hooves like those under you,
There would be sorrow in your eyes.'

And 'twas plain that he knew the sorrow so well
In the horse's eyes,
And he wondered so deeply that he dived in the end
Into the horse's mind.

I looked at the horse then that I might see
The sorrow in his eyes,
And Turnbull's eyes were looking at me
From the horse's mind.

I looked at Turnbull and looked once again
And there in Turnbull's head —
Not Turnbull's eyes, but, dumb with grief,
Were the horse's eyes instead.

from the Irish of Seán Ó Ríordáin
(1917–1977)

Brown Eyes

These brown eyes I see are hers
Now in her son's head,
It was a thing most beautiful
That you inherited;

It was a meeting privileged
With her mind and body too,
For a thousand years would pass so swift
If they but looked at you.

Because those eyes belong to her
It's strange that he has them,
I'm ashamed to face her now because
They happened in a man.

When she and they were one to me
Little did I think
Those eyes would change to masculine
That spoke so womanly.

Where is the source of madness
That's any worse than this?
Do I have to change my dialogue
Now that they are his?

She wasn't the first to see with them
Any more than he
Nor will he be the last
Who will wear them.

Is this all there is of eternity
That something of us lives on
Becoming masculine and feminine
From the mother to the son?

from the Irish of Seán Ó Ríordáin

Christmas Eve

With candles of angels the sky is now dappled,
The frost on the wind from the hills has a bite,
Kindle the fire and go to your slumber,
Jesus will lie in this household tonight.

Leave all the doors wide open before her,
The Virgin who'll come with the child on her breast,
Grant that you'll stop here tonight, Holy Mary,
That Jesus tonight in this household may rest.

The lights were all lighting in that little hostel,
There were generous servings of victuals and wine
For merchants of silk, for merchants of woollens
But Jesus will lie in this household tonight.

from the Irish of Máire Mhac an tSaoi
(b. 1922)

Captivity

I am an animal

a wild animal
from the tropics
      famous
      for my beauty

I would shake the trees of the forest
once
with my cry

but now
I lie down
and observe with one eye
the lone tree yonder

people come in hundreds
every day
who would do anything
for me
but set me free

from the Irish of Caitlín Maude
(1941–1982)

from The Purge

Hartnett, the poet, might as well be dead,
enmeshed in symbol — the fly in the web;
and November dribbles through the groves
and metaphors descend on him in droves:
the blood-sucked symbols — the sky so blue,
the lark, the kiss, and the rainbow too.
This syrupy drivel would make you puke.

The monarch now of an inch of vision,
I'll not fall down for indecision
but banish for now and forever after
the rusty hinges, the rotten rafters,
the symbols, the cant, the high allusion
that reduce the white mind to confusion.
Inspiration comes and the poet is left
with the empty rattle of discarded shells,
the husks of beetles piled up dead—
his poem spoiled by stupid talk
that sucks the blood of an ancient craft
like a bloated tick on a mongrel's balls.
I must purge my thought and flay my diction
or else suffer that fierce affliction —
my poems only wind and bombast
having lost their human language.

Pleasant the young poet's dance with books
but the old poet's advance should be rebuffed—
the mummer in the tinker's shawl,
the garrulous brass-thief, the jackdaw,
the beat-up chair at the carpenter's,
and the scabby mouths of idle whores.

Bad cess to him who first compared
the poet's rhymes to the singing bird—
he insulted plumage, he insulted verse.
May Egypt shit him from a swallow's arse...

Like mousefur in a cat's mouth
or a bloodclot seeking a brain,
the white myths are stalking
the old poets' veins:
Icarus, Meadbh and Christ—
yes, the Christ who died
to free the world of mythologies
is himself mythologised.
These are scabs of knowledge, and cankers in the groin,
the leeches of the soul sucking strong.
When we're tired and frightened
And when poetry dies
we plant the white ghosts in the scorched garden.
We believe that they're alive —
the dead forever dead, except in our silly minds...

I am the grave of hope and the tomb of truth,
swiller of fame, gulper of residues.
The systems of great men will never mend
my heart's drop-down, the leak of sentiment.
I construct myself with Plato's ears,
Hegel's thumb, Freud's beard,
Nietzsche's 'tache and Bergson's teeth
to make my body whole, complete.
I add Buddha to the crush
and Lao Tsu's teachings are a must:
but a pain in my belly upsets my powers
and my body explodes in a rain of flowers,
and down I come with a shower of poets—

oh, they're some flowers, these perfumed oafs
with juniper of Aristotle, bogcotton of Kant,
sage of Schopenhauer, arrogant.
Here in a wood among stem and branch
like a child lost at a hurling match,
I hear the cheering of lusty throats
and see only the hems of coats.
Oh, I am Frankenstein and his creature
made of spittle, and bits and pieces...

Imagine a world with nothing but poems,
desert-naked and bare-boned:
with nothing but swans and lilies and roses—
such a meagre fauna and flora.
All the foliage in technicolour,
dwarf and giant, joy and squalor.
If poets celebrate the world's soul
and the rare and wonderful they extol,
where's the mention of the plover?
Where's the nest of the water dipper?
If no bird sang but Philomel,
and nothing was but sunrise, sunset,
the world we live in would be hell.
We're the boys who adore freedom
wanting only the praise of people:
we're the boys who fatten geese
to swell their livers for our feast.
We lost the election for our party,
the rags we wear make tailors narky.
We promise you silk and we give you cotton,
we fill the world with wrens from top to bottom.

The poet is only his Collected Verse,
and all he was is contained in books:

His poetry is his true memorial —
other than that, mere fables and stories.
Our viaticum is knowledge
and death wants nothing from us
but ourselves and our knowledge.
The brave man spends knowledge freely
or else grows frightened, growing lonely;
and the straws fall that he stole from others —
his roof leaks on him. He shudders:
his bloated soul no more will hunger
and his once white mind is white no longer
and the thatch hardens, and the lights are smothered.
To die without knowledge of yourself
is the worst darkness, the worst hell:
to bequeath your truth to humanity
is the only immortality...

Statement is castrated verse —
a cry, a slogan — so we've heard:
the hymn of the pompous clerk.
Once our country was Róisín Dubh:
today it's a warlord, a stoat with a hood,
a sandy beach with an oil-soaked bird.
Of slogans now you can take your pick —
not poems or songs but rhetoric.
Where verse is treacherous, 'tis fitting and right
for the poet to turn fighter with an armalite.
A poem in prison isn't worth a fart —
won't dent a helmet, won't stop a shot:
won't feed a soul when the harvest rots,
won't put food in hungry pots.
Famine and war to all historians!
May popstars roar our ballads glorious!
Justice is the poet's land:

he has no family but a load
of dreams to sting, and coax, and goad
with words as worthless as tin cans.
May heavy boots stomp on the head
that forgets the danger of being understood...

A critic floundered in a poem once
for want of signposts, the poor dunce.
He crushed each subtlety underfoot
and wept, hearing their brittle crunch.
He prayed to God that he might see;
he invoked the ghosts of the University.
'Straight ahead,' came the blessed answer,
'to line twenty-nine, and look for Dante,'
and, released, he praised the poem, the chancer.
He saw no polish, or craft, or care
nor the subtle power of the poet aware—
only that ugly signpost there.
His compass was of no account
in a place that had no north or south.
What's a critic, in the name of Bridget,
or can any 'objective correlative' gauge it?

So, what is left when the piper ceases?
Dregs, spit, echoes, treacle.
There's still a problem, all said and done:
the poem that lives, will it be human?
I break my dictum — it's not a rule
but a harness on me, poetry's mule...

This is Ireland, and I'm myself.
I preach the gospel of non-assent.
Love and art is the work I want
as empty as a dipper's nest,

whiter than a goose's breast —
the poet's road with no milestone on it,
a road with no wayside stop upon it,
a road of insignificant herbs
welling quietly from every hedge.

from the Irish of Mícheál Ó hAirtnéide (Michael Hartnett)
(1941–1999)

Róisín Dubh: an allegorical name for Ireland (pronounce *Row-sheen Duv*)

A Braddy Cow

He got fed up, I'd swear,
of the loneliness that constantly seeps down
through the rolling hills, through the valleys
sluggish as a hearse;
of the lazy hamlets of the foothills
empty of youth as of earth;
of the old warriors, of the sodbusters
who turned to red-sod the peaty soil
and who deafened him pink, year-in, year-out,
bragging of the old sods of the past;

of the small, white bungalows, ugly
as dandruff in the sedgy headlands of the Glen;
of the young trapped in the cage of their fate
like wild animals who have lost their cunning;
of the three sorrows of storytelling in the misery
of the unemployed, of low spirits,
of the backwardness, of the narrowmindedness of both sides
      of the Glen,
of the fine birds below in Ruairí's
who stirred the man in him
but who couldn't care less about his lusting;

of tribal boundaries, of ancient household ditches,
of pissing his frustration at race and religion
that walled him in.
He got fed up of being fettered in the Glen
and, bucking like a braddy cow one spring morning,
he cleared the walls and hightailed away.

from the Irish of Cathal Ó Searcaigh
(b. 1956)

A braddy cow: (dialect) a thieving, trespassing cow

Her First Flight

'I love you, Dad! I love you!
I love this massive plane —
It looks like a big fat pencil case
(Aer Spain — is it, Dad? — Aer Spain?)

This aeroplane's exciting,
It's noise-ing up to go —
Will it drive as fast as you, Dad?
But Dad — we're going slow.'

*'We're driving to our runway, dear,
And then we'll go real fast —
Faster than even I drive.'*
'Whee, Dad! Whee! At last!

We're going really speedy,
When are we going to fly?
Wow! Up, up, up we go Dad!
'Way up in the sky.

What's happening to my ears Dad?
They're funny — I can't hear
(Well kind of); what you say, Dad?
There's something in my ears.'

*'Suck a sweet, 'twill help you —
It's a good idea.'*
'Who's *Eddie*, Daddy?' *'Eddie?'*
'I said it's a good idea.

*Look at the clouds now, Nessa:
We're coming to them — just;
In a minute we'll be through them.'*
'Dad! It's like they're made of dust—

The clouds are awful dusty,
I can't see a thing —
Just dark outside my window.
Now what's happening? —

We're above the clouds! The sunshine!'
'*Sit back now and relax.*
It's three hours to Tenerife —
Let's have a little nap.'

'Daddy, we're not moving —
Look down at the sea:
It's not moving, we're not moving,
This is boring — I have my wee!

Daddy, where's the toilet?
I'm bored with this oul' plane.'
'*Look out the window, Nessa —*
Look down and you'll see Spain.'

'Daddy, where's the toilet?
Is there any on this plane?'
'*OK, OK, I'll take you*';
'Daddy, we're over Spain...

When I was at the toilet,
I made poops as well as wee —
Where did the poops go, Daddy?
The poops I made, the wee?

Did they fall down on some Spanish man
'Way 'way down below?
Where did my poops go, Daddy?
Where did my wee-wee go?

What's next after Spain, Dad?
Will we get our dinner soon?
This aeroplane's exciting,
How far up is the moon?

Dad, my ears are popping —
Is everything all right?
Daddy, oops! — I chewed my sweet
I got such an awful fright.

But it's OK now Daddy —
It's just the plane going down.
Daddy, Daddy! Tenner Reef!
Dad, is this our town?'

Sonnet to Brenda

I won't compare you to a summer's day,
The beaches all deserted in the rain —
Some way, this, to spend a holiday
(You're sorry now you didn't book for Spain).
No! The weather can't be trusted in these parts —
It's fickle as a false love's said to be;
I could get sentimental about hearts
But that's not my style. Poetry,
The only thing that's constant in my life,
The only thing I know that still is true
As my love remains for you, dear wife —
This, then, is what I'll compare to you.
The iambic heart that pulses in these lines
Measures out my love. And it still rhymes.

A Song of Experience

for
Declan & Beth Kiberd

There are certain songs a singer cannot sing
Because roughness, or its lack, is in his voice.
What we get in life is what we bring.

A singer's of the earth or of the wing:
He's born that way; he has no other choice.
There are certain songs a singer cannot sing.

When we were young and revelled in its fling,
Attempting all and never thinking twice
(What we get in life is what we bring),

We thought that we were lords of everything;
In middle age, we now must pay the price:
There are certain songs a singer cannot sing.

The voice now has the depth of seasoning —
Let past excesses hold us in their vice,
What we get in life is what we bring;

And though the singing's better as we wring
A verse or two from all with which we diced,
There are certain songs a singer cannot sing.
What we get in life is what we bring.

Here, for once, I didn't pine for home:
This was a world where language altered all;
Here Irish fitted like a poem —
In school, 'twas just a subject; here you'd fall
In love with being Irish: you were free
To learn the words of love not taught in school;
Oh! Irish was that girl at the *Céilí* —
If you could only ask her out, not make a fool
Of yourself, and dance with her all night,
You'd learn the moods of Irish on her tongue;
She smiled at you, and oh! your head was light,
You danced with her and wheeled and waltzed and swung.
We danced all night, we didn't even kiss,
But this was love, was Irish, and was bliss.

Gaeltacht: (Irish) an Irish-speaking district; the state of being Irish
    (pronounce *Gale-tocked*)
Céilí: (Irish) an Irish dancing session (pronounce *Kay-lee*)

Dan Breen

'there's a great gap between a gallous story and a dirty deed'
The Playboy of the Western World

'My Fight for Irish Freedom' by Dan Breen —
I read it like a Western; I'd pretend
To be a freedom fighter at thirteen —
It made a change from 'Cowboys'; I'd spend
My spare time freeing Ireland in my head
Reliving his adventures one by one —
The policemen that he shot at Solohead,
Romance about the days spent on the run.

A nation born of romance and of blood,
Once ruled by men who killed for their beliefs,
Now a nation grown to adulthood
Losing faith in heroes, tribal chiefs.
Dan Breen is laid with the giants who held sway;
The gallous reads of dirty deeds today.

Gallous: a composite word incorporating *gallant*, *callous* and *gallows*

Knocklong

Oh, take me through the byroads
To those places named in song:
Along the road less travelled
Is the station of Knocklong
Where shots rang out for freedom
In nineteen and nineteen
With young Seán Hogan rescued
By Seán Treacy and Dan Breen.

As I drive to Tipperary
I recall the lore,
The War of Independence—
Here I park my car
On a road become a songline
And walk into the song
The Rescue of Seán Hogan
At the Station of Knocklong.

The station's now deserted,
Blocked up, overgrown
But not the gallous story,
An empire overthrown;
But I am overtaken
By the traffic on the road
Who hoot at this obstruction,
The progress I have slowed.

And so I take the burden
Of history and drive
Into Tipperary
Where I see New Ireland thrive;

But I'm glad I took the byroad
That lead me into song —
Many roads to Tipperary
But only one Knocklong.

Just my Luck I'm not Pig-ignorant

Just my luck I'm not pig-ignorant
Though it's bad to be a boor
Now that I have to go out among
This miserable shower.

A pity I'm not a stutterer,
Good people, among you
For that would suit you better,
You thick, ignorant crew.

If I found a man to swap, I'd trade
Him verses that would cheer —
As good a cloak as would come, he'd find,
Between him and despair.

Since a man is less respected
For his talent than his suit,
I regret that what I've spent on art
I haven't now in cloth.

Since happy the words and deeds that show no hint,
On boorish tongues, of music, metre, clarity,
I regret the time I've wasted grappling with hard print
Since my prime, that I didn't spend it on vulgarity.

A translation of 'Mairg nach fuil 'na dhubhthuata'
by Dáibhí Ó Bruadair (c.1625–1698)

A Teacher Sings the Blues

I've never found the time
To indulge the child within —
All day I'm teaching children.
There are times I could give in

It's so lonely in the classroom,
And the kids don't understand
That I, too, hurt like they do;
And my! how kids can wound.

At lunch time I'm 'on duty',
I patrol the shrill school yard
A sandwich and a cuppa
In my hand. Oh, it's so hard

To keep an eye on children,
And if one of them gets hurt
You wonder if they'll sue you
And you've never been in court.

And the kids are getting bolder
And you know this could be good
'Cos, a child, you'd no such freedom,
You did as you were told.

And when you retire on pension
With forty years put in
They'll make a Presentation
In the local *Arms* or *Inn*;

And you'll look back, if you're lucky,
On a job, you hope, well done.
Then shortly you're forgotten —
You know that life moves on.

A Parent's Love

How close the sound of laughter and of tears!
My children watching *Dumbo* on TV
In the next room — are those wails or cheers?
At this remove their screaming worries me.

Do my children laugh or cry in the next room?
I check them out, and this is what I see—
No light illuminates the falling gloom,
Instead of watching *Dumbo* on TV,

High jinks on the sofa — they're both well,
I tick them off, their giggles fill and burst;
A parent's love knows all it needs of hell—
I hear them play and strangely fear the worst.

In the Attic

You're going up in the attic, Dad —
Please can I come too?
I'll even get the ladder, Dad,
And put it up for you.

Of all the places in our house
I love the attic best;
It's dark there — dark as Christmas
With every box a chest

Of surprise and promise —
The things we store up there
Are put away like memories
To open if you dare.

You're going up in the attic, Dad —
Can I come up too, please!
For hidden in the attic
Among the memories

Is part of me and part of you —
The part we seldom show;
Oh, up there in the attic, Dad,
Is all we're not, below.

Listening to *Desperados Waiting for a Train*

for
John

How one thing always leads us to another!
I see you with your grandad once again
As you walk off from your father and your mother
To join him in the world of grown-up men.
And yes, son, local folk called you his sidekick
As you walked around the village hand in hand,
No babytalk, 'twas adult stuff like politics
And it felt good to be treated like a man.
And though Grandad's dead and everything is changing,
And you're growing up and soon will leave us, son,
And life's a past we're always rearranging,
When the kid walks with his hero in that song
I see you with your grandad once again
As you walk away to join the world of men.

A Wrenboy's Farewell

for Maurice Heffernan
& the Moyvane Wrenboys

Farewell to Winter madness, Summer larks,
The show is over, we're back on firm land;
No more our torches will light up the dark,
The time has come and now we must disband.
Farewell to music, singing, dancing, rhymes,
The public show of all we are about,
This pageant that we dreamed in other times—
The show is over. Put the torches out.
The old are weary, wise in their defeat,
The young protest and wonder if they can
Revive the glory, again march down the street
Under the proud banner of Moyvane.
Go home. The show is over. The banner's furled.
We walk back up the street into the world.

Batt Mannon

Batt Mannon is our hamster,
Spends all his time awake
Gnawing at his cage bars
Attempting to escape.

But steel will not be broken
By the strongest jaws,
And yet he keeps on trying.
Is this because

The hamster has no memory,
Or, too stupid to give in,
He's torn by no depression,
Hope his greatest sin?

Whatever — he keeps gnawing
Till pity frees him for
A few hard-earned minutes
To run around the floor.

He understands no pity.
The hamster is his jaws —
He thinks they've won him freedom.
This is his reward.

He gnaws the bars that hold him
All his hours awake.
Only we who pity
Know there's no escape.

The Well

I heard it of a winter's night
In childhood, years ago
When tales were told to keep the cold
Outside with the wind and snow

How once upon a moonlit night
A piper passed this way
Coming from a *céilí*
In the parish of Athea

And as he walked he whistled
A tune, a merry tune
And the only other sound that night
Was howling at the moon.

He walked along the fairy path
Whistling his merry tune
When suddenly a darkness
Stole across the moon

And all the dogs fell silent
As he came upon the well
And a voice from the waters spoke to him
And this is what befell:

There's some call it glaucoma
And some the fairies' curse
For when he woke next morning
Beside the fairy bush

He was blind; and ever after
He would never tell
What the voice of the waters whispered
From the fairy well.

The fairies are no longer
And all their wanton harm,
And the well supplies fresh water
Piped up to a farm,

And when I ask the old man
Who told the tale to me
If he believes in fairies
He says, 'I don't believe

In fairies',
And turns to face me then:
'No! I don't believe in fairies.
But I'm afraid of them.'

Geronimo

for
Kathleen Cain

Here, *tiswin* and Apaches didn't mix —
The White Eyes banned its brewing, just in case:
Drunk, Apaches could be lunatics,
They'd get out of their heads and wreck the place —
The place the White Eyes sent them when they took
Their land, their homes, their way of life, to live
As the White Eyes told them — by *their* book.
Geronimo got drunk; a fugitive,
He jumped the Reservation with his band
(He broke the law, and soon would pay the price),
Returned to his home, familiar land —
Sober, perhaps, he'd have considered twice,
Ignored a truth; but, drunk, Geronimo,
A warrior again, knew he should go.

tiswin: Apache corn beer

Ode to a Pint of Guinness

'An Buachaill Caol Dubh', *'The Blonde in the Black Skirt'* —
You have given me life which I'd never have known,
For I was the shy one, inward and lonesome,
Fearful of people the years I was growing.

You came to me first in the years I was courting—
No girl would stay with me on lemonade;
You gave me fine words and a high reputation
For romance and laughter. At last I was made!
You came to me sad and you came to me happy—
There were parts of myself that lay unexplored,
But thanks to you, Guinness, there's nothing within us
That doesn't come out in thought, deed or word.

There are two kinds of truth, one drunk and one sober—
The ancient Egyptians knew this very well;
Before they'd pronounce, they'd examine it both ways—
The kind of good counsel I'd bottle and sell.

How different my life would be measured without you—
An egghead, I fear, with his nose in a book;
But now I can scan the pulse of my people
And the scholars will read it to get one last look
At the village before it has lost its own story,
The last place on earth for the wild and the free,
Ere we turn to designer beers, *Beautiful Bodies!*,
And we speak like bad actors speak on TV.

So here's to you, Guinness, muse and confuser—
You brought me to visions, you brought me to fart:
All the pain that you caused me was nothing at all, love,
To the knowledge you taught to this once-sober heart!

An Buachaill Caol Dubh: (Irish) 'The Dark Slender Boy', a synonym for
   alcohol from the song of the same name by Seán Aerach Ó Seanacháin
   (mid-eighteenth century) (pronounce *Un Boo-kill Kay-ul Duv*.)

The Woman of the House

The village — Ballygariff
Sometime in the past
Where the clock advanced for Closing Time
Is the only thing that's fast.

In her pub, Maggie Browne
(Browne's her maiden name)
Serves pints and whiskies to a group
Who've recently come home

On holiday from England,
They wear their Sunday best —
They're out to prove that exile
Does better than the rest

Who stay at home in Bally
And work that windswept hill
And so they dress in Sunday best
And flash big *twenty* bills.

Enter then Tom Guiney,
The singer, for a beer;
He's bought tobacco for himself,
Sugar, tea and flour

For his wife above in Barna,
He comes in for 'just the one'
But the exiles stand him porter
And demand of him a song.

All afternoon he sings for them;
At 'The Home I Left Behind'
The exiles back in Bally
Stare into black pints

For song is all that's left them
Of Bally long ago,
The past is all that's left them,
The only home they know.

Tom Guiney, man of honour,
Will stand his round
Though what's left in his pocket
Would hardly make a pound.

Nonetheless he calls for
A drink for the company —
'Twould never be said in Bally
He drank all day for free.

Maggie Browne sets up the drinks
And Tom must now admit
That he hasn't enough to pay for them —
Could she put it on the slate?

She does. And on with singing
But Maggie bides her time
And in a private moment
Takes Tom aside.

'Tom,' she says, 'You'll never
Call for a drink again
With no money in your pocket
For a crowd like them.

Call for your drink, Tom Guiney,
And when I put it up
If you've no money in your pocket
Let them take a sup

Or two and let them talk
And then come up to me
And ask me for the change
Of the *fiver* you gave me;

And Guiney, boy, you'll get it —
Never, never again
Let on that you've no money
To a crowd like them.'

The village — Ballygariff.
Time — the present. Now
We come to bury Maggie Browne;
We take and drink our stout —

We do this in memory
Of a woman we well know,
Exalter of the humble
In a singer long ago.

For Pat Coughlan

I walked back to *An Cúinne* to my past —
A pub I'd played in half a life ago
Those summers, a student, for the gas
(For nothing but the chance to do a show).
I walked into a card game where the players
Ignored me, as they should, to play their game;
'Twas Holy Thursday after church and prayers —
Would no one in *An Cúinne* know my name?

I saw him at the bar, alone, ignored —
Pat Coghlan, the musician, my old friend;
He took my hand, and out of him there poured
Mouth music — jigs and polkas without end.
It's as if I never left the place at all:
The music lives, its back against the wall.

Feed the World

A people for whom art means less than nothing,
Who'd post a notice in this church with pins
Stuck into the wood of *The Last Supper*
Will laugh at me. Still I condemn this sin.

They're doing good, collecting; and this notice
Is for hunger in the Third World — charity.
What matter if it's pinned on *The Last Supper*?
Who objects except a crank like me?

And so, blindly, they'll dismiss my accusation
For beauty won't put food in hungry mouths.
'Not by bread alone...'; it's useless to remind them.
(Affluence is, too, a kind of drought.)

A people for whom beauty's less than nothing
Will destroy not just a sculpture but the air,
Then turn to God to work his magic for them
And continue as before the latest scare.

And the lilies of the field are slowly dying,
And the sparrows of the air are poisoned too
Because good sticks pins on such as *The Last Supper*
And those who see are trumped by those who do.

Feed the world — we must; it is our duty;
No one is absolved who lets it starve,
But what is good without its source in beauty
Revealed here in the wood the sculptor carved?

A people for whom art means less than nothing,
Christians who are kind as they are true,
A Christ impaled with pins of human kindness:
'Forgive them for they know not what they do.'

My People

1. Jimmy Nolan

Jimmy Nolan, grocer, typed my name,
The printed word, just like it was in books;
Back then, the printed word was fame,
I'd hold it up and look, and look, and look.
He took photos, too, of weddings around here,
Anything to earn an honest bob
(A wooden leg, his walk a little queer),
He'd show the snaps to Mam — another job
Well done, he courted praise ('twas all he sought);
He wrote the local *Notes* and that was power,
He made the news from stories that were brought
By locals who would purchase tea and flour.
He typed us up, and every week we'd scan
Our inch of glory in *The Kerryman*.

2. Billy Cunningham

He told me that my singing was the equal
Of a goat pissing into a tin can.
Dismissed in youth! The story has a sequel —
He gave me songs when I grew a man,
The old songs that he learned from local rhymers
Who sang their place in triumph and defeat;
I'd spend evenings by his range with that old timer
And all who cared to drop in from the street.
Sitting there in Uncle Billy's kitchen
Where neighbours walked once more beyond the grave
And youngsters smoked first fags and spoke of mitching
As Billy took out his teeth to sing a stave,
The past would come alive upon his breath.
In circles such as these there is no death.

3. 'Old Jack Fitz'

'Old Jack Fitz', my Grandad, was a stern
Lover of perfection in his work.
His family, from early on, would learn
To harvest all their springs and never shirk.
They got on well in England and the States;
They danced their way through London in the War;
Their children come to Ireland, we're best mates:
I sing the old songs for them in the bar —
The songs his fellow farmers nightly sang
When Grandad and Nano would open up
Their *céilí* house and all the rafters rang
As neighbours came to sing and dance and sup
Where a lover of perfection could relax
Knowing the hay was saved, the oats in stacks.

4. Dad

A man before his time, he cooked and sewed,
Took care of me — and Mammy in her bed,
Stayed in by night and never hit the road.
I remember well the morning she was dead
(I'd been living up in Arklow — my first job,
I hit the road in patches coming home),
He came down from her room, began to sob
'Oh Gabriel, Gabriel, Gabriel, Mam is gone.'
He held me and I told him not to cry
(I loved her too, but thought this not the place—
I went up to her room, cried softly 'Why?'
Then touched her head quite stiffly, no embrace).
Now when the New Man poses with his kid,
I think of all the things my father did.

5. Mam

My mother wrote the meanings of hard words
In the margins of the books she'd recommend;
I coasted through those stories, and was stirred
By fantasy and romance: I'd pretend
To be what I was reading, made my bike
A cowboy horse, a hurley for a gun,
Picked a branch of hazel for a Vik-
ing spear; I'm sure she wondered at her son
Living out a fiction she'd prepared;
Her intention was to educate,
To spare me from a shop where, if you dared
To speak your mind, customers might 'migrate'.
A grocer's wife, wary of romance,
She bought those books, and I should take my chance.

6. Mick

Looking at your photo as a boy,
I see you now at eighty still unbowed,
That couldn't-care-less look still in your eye,
The kind of look that stands out from the crowd.
That photo shows a soul who'd travel light,
Who'd never bind himself to any school,
Whose only use for money — that he might
Enjoy a drink with friends upon a stool.

Uncle Mick, you're all I'll never be,
You have no need of what the world can give;
A bachelor, you live with family,
In England all those years you lived in digs.
Home for you is simply what you are
Who never owned a house or drove a car.

7. The Sandhills of Yamboorah

By the Sandhills of Yamboorah, a book I read
When I was twelve or thirteen, 'way back when
I'd take a book and sneak off into bed
And read all day of heroes — mostly men.
But this was different: the pace was easy, slow —
As Australia itself, or so I guessed;
The boy (he wasn't named) just seemed to know
His time, his place were suited to him best.
Australia! where no Lancelot would roam,
Just an old black man who helped the boy with chores —
Much the same as the life I led at home,
A life which, some complain, is stagnant, bores.
I read that book; in time I'd learn to say
The heroes live beside me, day by day.

In Memory of My Mother

My mother lived for books though nearly blind.
An invalid, she read while she could see.
The only pleasure left her was her mind.

The books she read that pleased her were designed
To strip her life down to a clarity.
My mother lived for books though nearly blind

While I'd read all the comics I could find;
Confined to bed, she'd read 'good books' to me.
The only pleasure left her was her mind.

Delighting in the vision of her kind,
That second sight, the gift of poetry,
My mother lived for books though nearly blind,

Books I read from bookshelves that were lined
With poems she'd recite from memory.
The only pleasure left her was her mind.

And I remembered as I launched and signed
The first slim *Poems* of my maturity
How Mammy lived for books though nearly blind,
The only pleasure left to her, her mind.

So What if There's No Happy Ending?

in memoriam
Michael Hartnett

So what if there's no happy ending?
Don't be afraid of the dark;
Open the door into darkness
And hear the black dogs bark.

Oh what a wonder is darkness!
In it you can view
The moon and stars of your nature
That daylight hid from you.

Open the door into darkness,
There's nothing at all to fear —
Just the black dogs barking, barking
As the moon and stars appear.

I Have Seen My People, Soon to Die

I have seen my people, soon to die,
Battling death with a wasting act of will —
They linger on, drugged up to the eyes
With morphine which relieves but also kills.
Ah yes, I've seen them in and out of sense
In hospice beds, in rest homes where they lie
Attended by relations who, growing tense,
Break down and pray their loved ones die.
And still they linger, confounding all that's known
Of cancer and the ways that it can kill;
They whisper that they want to die at home
But all in vain, they're in their railed beds still.
And you watch them and there's nothing you can do.
And you know that this could also happen you.

Dick

When Dick came home to Applegarth to die
(Two weeks, they told me in the hospital),
He faced the truth that no-one can deny.

He must have known 'twas up, yet didn't cry —
He cried in private if he cried at all
When Dick came home to Applegarth to die.

At night when friends and neighbours would drop by
To live the past, talk up a festival,
He faced the truth that no-one can deny.

Every day he'd send me out to buy
The fags he knew that were his funeral
When Dick came home to Applegarth to die;

For in dying, as in life, he wasn't shy —
To the end, he'd hold me still in thrall;
He faced the truth that no-one can deny,

A cancer that would kill but not destroy;
He came to me when he heard death's call,
When Dick came home to Applegarth to die
And faced the truth that no-one can deny.

God Bless the Child

God bless the child that never grew to life,
Our dead embryo — not even a stillbirth—
Detached inside its mother's womb. My wife
And I can't even give it to the earth
From which life comes, returning it to dust.
I'll light a candle for it; on second thought,
I won't. I can't — to do so would be just
A sentimental gesture, a bouquet bought
At Reception on visiting my wife,
A silent touch perhaps to bring relief;
No candles then, I seek the words of life
That one, perhaps, might fertilize our grief.
Now every word upon my lips is prayer
Pregnant with the life that we must bear.

To Jack Kerouac

'The only people for me are the mad ones,
the ones who are mad to live, mad to talk,
mad to be saved, desirous of everything at
the same time, the ones who never yawn or
say a commonplace thing but burn,
burn like fabulous yellow roman candles'

On the Road

Leafing through your books tonight, a breeze of memory from
every page,
My youth was resurrected, and, rising in me, I felt the dreamy
beat that imitated you in the early 'seventies.
1973. I was hooked on you. Day after day, your work was a
shot of inspiration that lit up my mind and stretched my
imagination.
Then it wasn't *Mín 'a Leá* or *Fána Bhuí* I'd see but the plains
of Nebraska or the grasslands of Iowa.
And when the blues descended it wasn't the *Bealtaine* byways
that lay ahead but the open freeway of America.
'Hey man you gotta stay high' I'd say to my friend as we
freaked through *Cill Ulta's* California to *Fál Charrach's*
Frisco.

Your book is shut on my breast but beneath the skin that is the
cover your heart is throbbing in the muscle of every word.
Oh man! I feel it again, those highs on the Himalayas of youth:
From coast to coast we coasted, naive, vivacious, reckless
Hitch-hiking on our pilgrimage from New York to Frisco and
from there to Mexico City,
A mad beat to our lives. Inspired. Bombing down highways in
hot Cadillacs, bombed out of our minds on Benzedrine.
We crossed borders and broke through to dreams.
We celebrated every turn on our life's highway, binges and

brotherhood from Brooklyn to Berkeley, booze, bop and Buddhism; the sages of Asia; envelopes from eternity on the Sierras; marijuana and mysticism in Mexico; crazy visions in Bixby Canyon.

We made an Orpheus of every orifice.

Oh I remember it all, Jack, the talk and the quest.
You were the quickeyed bard on the road seeking perfection, seeking Heaven.
And though there's no shortcut to the Gods, so they say, you harnessed and electrified the Niagara of your mind with dope and divinity
And in that furious moment a light was generated that granted you a glimpse of eternity
And that guided you home, I hope, on the day of your death, to Whitman, Proust and Rimbaud.

My own road is ahead of me ... *'a road that ah zigzags all over creation. Yeah man! Ain't nowhere else it can go. Right!*
And some day on the road of old age and rheumatism,
Or sooner maybe,
I'll arrive at the Crossroads of Fate, and Death will be there before me,
A gentle guide to lead me beyond the border
And then, goddammit Jack, we'll both be hitch-hiking in eternity.

from the Irish of Cathal Ó Searcaigh

Mín 'a Leá: a placename (pronounce *Meen a Laa*)
Fána Bhuí: a placename (pronounce *Fauna Wee*)
Cill Ulta: a placename (pronounce *Kill Ulta*)
Fál Charrach: a placename (pronounce *Fall Kor-agh*)

Requiescat

He shouldered Mammy's coffin
And I was at his side,
A strong man in his fifties;
More than Mammy died

As we lowered her coffin,
My childhood ended then
As I stood beside my father
At her grave among the men.

We shouldered other coffins
These twenty years and more,
My father strong and steady
Though our shoulders would be sore.

And even last October
When his sister Nora died,
At eighty years he shouldered her
Still steady by my side.

He shouldered no more coffins—
When my aunt Mary died
And we went to lift her coffin,
My father stood aside.

His hand upon her coffin,
He followed up the aisle,
My father still beside me
Awhile.

His brothers now too feeble
To lift his coffin when
My father died, we wheeled him,
Myself and those old men.

And as we lowered you, father,
A generation knew
That the time had come for passing on.
Now I inherit you.

X on a tree trunk
Marks no buried treasure here
Children wonder why

*

A rotting tree stump
In the middle of the woods
Mushrooms with new life

*

Where there are nettles
There are dock leaves to heal us
In a spot nearby

Big Con

for my dear friend
Con Greaney, singer

Big Con lives in the mountain
In a thatched house on his own,
His wife is dead fifteen years,
His family, long grown,

Have left the ancestral mountain
But Con will not remove:
His life is in the mountain,
His love.

Born on the mountain
These eighty years and more,
Not *born* so much as quarried;
The mountain life was poor

('Twas Rooska of the curlew),
But not poor of heart —
He came from singing people
Whose life was art.

Big Con, King of singers
Has songs that only he
Brought from the singing people.
He sang his songs for me.

*

Once upon an emptiness
The Lost Man came home —
The man was lost because
He had lost his song.

— 134 —

He searched everywhere but couldn't find it
(Did he ever have the song?
He wondered)
So he collected songs.

He went to the oldest singers,
He learned all their songs,
He sang them for his people
But still did not belong.

One night, he sang with Donie Lyons,
A farmer out of Glin,
A flute player and singer.
Donie said to him:

'There's an old man in the West Limerick Hills
That no-one remembers now;
He might have what you're looking for.'
They finished their pints of stout;

They bought beer and whiskey
As an offering to Big Con
And drove into the mountain.
Would the giant sing his songs?

'Ye're welcome as the flowers of May,'
Beamed Big Con, 'Come in!
How're you keeping, Donie?
How're ye all in Glin?'

'Fine, Con,' replied Donie;
'Con, I brought this man,
He's recorded many singers,
He's looking for a song.'
'If I have the song, he'll get it;
Make yereselves at home.'

We drank a few throws of whiskey,
Knocked back a couple of beers
Then Con exploded into song.
The Lost Man, startled, hears

Him bend the air and twist it —
An old life made anew,
And every time 'twas different
And every time 'twas true,
The song that he was looking for,
The self that he once knew.

*

We break for beer and whiskey
And then return to song,
And song turns to story:
The story is Big Con...

*'I remember my time in England,
Times were bad 'round here;
I had to leave my wife and children
In Rooska for a year.*

*I took the boat for England,
Met my brother at the quay —
He brought me home to Huddersfield,
Looked for work for me.*

*A few days I lived off him
And then one night he said
"There's a job going with the darkies —
I'd be careful of that crowd."*

*But I worked away with the black men,
They were the same as me —
They found me strange, I found them strange;
We worked silently*

Until one day my partner
Forgot to bring his lunch —
He was leaving the job at dinner hour
For what you'd now call 'brunch'.

'There's no need to go,' I told him,
'I have plenty for us here';
I gave him half my sandwiches;
After work we went for beer.

And here was I — someplace —
Black men all around;
They stood to me all evening,
Wouldn't let me stand a round.

And what was it but a sandwich,
Pan loaf that made a friend?
They drove me home at Closing Time;
My brother was out of his mind:

"Jeezus, I thought they'd killed you —
In that place at night;
You don't know where you're going."
"Them people is all right,"

I told him.
"I'm welcome there, they said,
And the reason that I'm welcome
Is I gave a black man bread."

And one day in the woollen mill,
A bale fell on my foot,
I was going to the doctor
But my partner said, "No good! —

You no go to doctor,
Him take you off the job,
We do your work till you better,
You no lose a bob."

So I turned up each morning
And the black men did my work,
We went for beer each evening
And I'd go home after dark.

And the night before I was leaving
I spent it with the blacks;
They were singing their songs
And one said in the jacks:

"Big Con, you have your own songs?"
I told him I could sing
But they wouldn't know my singing;
Still, they made me sing.

I sang the songs the mountain sang
At Feast and Fast and Fair
And d'you know, 'twas like the mountain
Had removed from here to there.

We drank all night, we said goodbye,
We'd never meet again;
I took the boat next evening,
Went back to bogs and drains.'

*

At peace at last, the Lost Man
Sent Con's songs throughout the land
And the legend grew with the singers
Who sought out this old man...

'There's a Concert up in Dublin, Con;
Everyone will be there;
Will you come and sing your songs for us
Pure as mountain air?'

On the night of the big Concert,
His first time so far from home
Since he returned from Huddersfield,
We gazed around our room

(I'd travelled to Dublin with him —
He needed me, he said;
He didn't know Dublin
And I did).

A hotel room, *en suite*, TV,
But Con got bored with that,
He took off downstairs to find the bar
For a pint, a pipe and chat.

Who is this old singer
They're putting on tonight?
An old man from the mountains.
Can he do it here? He might...

The MC shepherds Big Con
Backstage from the bar:
'Con,' he chides, 'this is no pub,
This stage is for stars —

You can't just start up singing,
You must talk first to the crowd;
Do you think, Con, you can do it?'
Con just laughs out loud —

'I see the Pope in Galway
When he said Mass on the TV —
He told the crowd he loved them;
Don't worry about me.'

'*Ladies and gentlemen, Big Con*'
Silence, a polite clap,
And Con saunters out on stage
With his pint and cap.

He remembers the Pope in Galway
As he faces the dark Hall —
'People of Dublin, I loves ye!'
The whole place is enthralled;

He sings six songs, his quota,
But the crowd cries out for more,
And when he's finished singing,
They clap till their hands are sore.

*

Big Con and the Lost Man
Travel home by train,
And the Lost Man says to Big Con,
'I won't see your like again.'

Over in the West Limerick Hills
In a thatched house with his dog,
Big Con lives, a giant.
If his life was one hard slog

Now they come throughout the land
To learn at his feet —
'*Ye're welcome as the flowers of May*'
I hear an old man greet.

A Giant Never Dies

in memoriam Michael Hennessy
of Moyvane & Ballyduff

'I come from sweet Knockauling,
John Bradley is my name
And I'm the king of hurlers
For hurling is my game.'

So sang young John Bradley
As he dashed from the TV
His head full of hurling,
Great deeds and bravery

On that Sunday in September,
All Ireland Hurling Day,
The All-Ireland Final over;
He dashed outside to play

With a hurling stick and rubber ball,
He hurled on his own —
He'd no brothers or no sisters
And so he played alone

Whack! against the gable
Then run and leap and catch
Re-playing the All-Ireland,
Making it his match.

And then, his mind-game over,
He ran in home to Dad
And they talked of hurling heroes
And the mighty games they played.

Dad told him of the exploits
Of Big Mick Hennessy
Who played football for Knockauling
And hurling for Ballylee;

And how once upon a Championship
He was called to play
In the local Football Final
And on that selfsame day

When the football match was over
He played for Ballylee
In the County Hurling Final
In the great Park of Tralee.

In the centre for Knockauling,
He scored five points that day
And when the match was over
He left the field of play,

No time to celebrate and lift
The cup of victory —
He dashed out to the hackney car
That would take him to Tralee
And changed Knockauling's colours
For the green of Ballylee.

Just in time for the second half,
His team a goal behind,
Big Mick Hennessy took the field
And hurled into the wind;

And when the game was over
He'd scored three goals to win
And thousands knew they'd never see
The likes of him again.

The time is some weeks later,
The place — the Park, Tralee,
The County Hurling Final,
Tullybeg and Ballylee.

John Bradley and his Daddy
Have travelled here this day,
A treat for young John's birthday —
Eleven years today.

The game is fast and factious,
And at half time they see
The men of forty years ago,
Knockane and Ballylee,

As thirty men in suits walk out,
The hurlers of that day
When Big Mick Hennessy showed to all
How the great can play;

And as his name is called out
Each man waves to the crowd
And at the name 'Mick Hennessy'
The cheers are long and loud.

But young John Bradley's puzzled —
The man he sees out there
Is not as he imagined:
With glasses, thinning hair,

To young John he looks no different
From the other men
Standing out there on the field.
He realises then

That Mick Hennessy's a story
Of a giant with a ball
And what he sees there on the field
Is not a giant at all.

Yes, Mick Hennessy's a story —
One that will be told
When Big Mick is dead and gone
And young John Bradley's old.

For a giant lives in story
Among his people who
Believe in deeds of greatness
And honour all that's true.

Yes, Mick Hennessy's our story,
A giant with a ball
Who once upon a Championship
Won glory for us all.